Barbara Ker Wilson is a well-known reviewer and writer,
with a long-standing interest in folklore. Her collections of folktales
include *Scottish Folktales and Legends* (Oxford University Press),
Tales Told to Kabbarli (Angus and Robertson) and *The Turtle and the Island*
(Hodder and Stoughton), in which this story first appeared.
Her other titles for Frances Lincoln include
Wishbones, illustrated by Meilo So.
Barbara Ker Wilson lives in Queensland, Australia.

Frané Lessac began her career as a painter on the Caribbean
island of Montserrat. She has illustrated over 20 books, including
Queen Esther Saves Her People by Rita Golden Gelman (Scholastic);
O Christmas Tree written by Vashanti Rahaman and *The Distant Talking Drum*
by Isaac Olaleye (both Boyd's Mill Press); and *On the Same Day in March*:
A Tour of the World's Weather written by Marilyn Singer (HarperCollins).
For Frances Lincoln she has illustrated Eric Maddern's *The Fire Children*,
which was selected as one of *Junior Education's* Best Books of the Year
in 1993 and as one of the Children's Books of the Year in 1994.
Frané Lessac lives in Freemantle, Australia.

For Mom and Dad
F.L.

The Turtle and the Island © Frances Lincoln Limited 1990
This story first appeared in a collection, *The Turtle and the Island,* published by
Hodder & Stoughton Australia, 1978.
It is based on a legend collected in Papua New Guinea by Donald Stokes.

Text © Barbara Ker Wilson and Donald Stokes 1978
Illustrations © Frané Lessac 1990

First published in Great Britain in 1990 by
Frances Lincoln Limited, 4 Torriano Mews
Torriano Avenue, London NW5 2RZ

British Library Cataloguing in Publication Data available on request.

ISBN 0-7112-0697-X paperback

Set in Infant Character Baskerville by Rowland

Printed in China

9 8

THE
TURTLE
AND THE
iSLAND

A FOLK TALE FROM PAPUA NEW GUINEA

WITH PAINTINGS BY FRANÉ LESSAC
STORY RETOLD BY BARBARA KER WILSON

FRANCES LINCOLN

Long, long ago, in the days when turtles had teeth, there lived a great sea-turtle, the mother of all sea-turtles, who spent her time swimming about the wide sea that now people call the Pacific Ocean.

Slowly she swam, feeding on the fishes that lived in the sea and the plants that grew there, and snapping up the shellfishes that lurked in the rocks where the sea bordered the land. She swam from one side of the sea to the other, to and fro between the lands that bordered that vast ocean.

She lived in the sea, but she swam both above and below the surface of the water. Above the surface she breathed the clear, fresh air and felt the warmth of the sun. She looked up to the sky and saw the sun by day and the moon by night, and the birds that flew across the ocean from land to land. She looked down into the sea and saw its dark, cold depths.

Sometimes the turtle grew tired of swimming, and rested just below the surface of the sea, but she often longed to rest in the warmth and sunshine. She thought how pleasant it would be if only there were a piece of land in the middle of the great ocean where she lived.

In a dark, secret cave far below the sea where the turtle swam there lived a man, and in all that great ocean he was the only man. He had no wife, no children, no tribespeople. The man was lonely, in that cave beneath the sea. His heart was heavy as a stone on the seashore. He was weary of being alone.

One day, as the turtle swam about, she came to a place
in the middle of the ocean where a great hill of sand was
raised up from the bottom of the sea. The hill was so
high that the top of it almost reached above the surface
of the ocean.

"If I were to bring more sand to add to this big hill, soon it would rise clear above the water," thought the turtle. "The sun would shine down upon it by day, and it would be a place where I could rest and enjoy the warmth and the clear air when I grow tired of swimming."

So the turtle went to another part of the ocean floor,
where she dug up rocks and more sand, and these she
brought back to the hill, so that it grew higher and
higher. She did this more times than anyone could
count. The sun rose and set, the moon waxed and waned
day after day, and still the hill grew higher. And at last
it became a huge island in the middle of the sea, and the
turtle saw that her work was finished.

Then the birds that flew across the ocean from land to land brought seeds of plants and trees and dropped them on the island. Grasses and flowering plants and tall trees sprang up, covering the rocks and sand. It was a beautiful, fertile island, surrounded by the sea which teemed with fishes large and small.

The turtle rested on the sun-warmed ground of the island she had made. No longer did she have to spend her whole life swimming through the wide ocean and resting just below its surface. And although she still swam about as before, she never strayed very far from the island she had made.

One day she swam down, down into the ocean, much deeper than she had ever swum before. How dark and cold it was down there, far from the light and warmth of the sun!

Suddenly the turtle swam into the dark, secret cave where the man had lived alone for such a long time. The man was overjoyed when the turtle came to him; he begged her to find him a wife who would be his companion and bear children. The turtle felt pity for the man's loneliness. She took him, riding on her strong shell, to the island she had made.

Then she swam across the sea to the nearest land, to a place where a woman stood on the shore, a beautiful woman. She was weeping; like the man, she was lonely. She desired a husband and longed to bear children. So the turtle took the woman back across the sea to the island, and brought her as a wife for the man.

The man and the woman lived together on the island in happiness and peace. They laughed, they played in the sea, sometimes they quarrelled, but they never lost the joy in their hearts.

They made children together, beautiful children, and those children had more children, and in this way the island became filled with people, who grew crops and built houses and fished along the seashore.

And in time the island that the great sea-turtle had
made became known as Papua New Guinea.

MORE PICTURE BOOKS IN PAPERBACK
FROM FRANCES LINCOLN

THE FIRE CHILDREN
Retold by Eric Maddern
Illustrated by Frané Lessac

Why are some people black, some white, and others yellow, pink and brown?
This intriguing West African creation myth tells how the first spirit-people
solve their loneliness using clay and fire – and fill the Earth
with children of every colour under the sun!

Suitable for National Curriculum English – Reading, Key Stages 1 and 2
Scottish Guidelines English Language – Reading, Levels B and C; Environmental Studies – Level C

ISBN 0-7112-0885-9 £5.99

WISHBONES
Barbara Ker Wilson
Illustrated by Meilo So

Wishbones, magic fishbones that make every dream come true…
From China comes this enchanted fable of a golden-eyed fish,
a lost slipper and a king's search for his bride.

Suitable for National Curriculum English – Reading, Key Stages 1 and 2
Scottish Guidelines English Language – Reading, Levels B and C

ISBN 0-7112-1415-8 £5.99

THE COMING OF NIGHT
James Riordan
Illustrated by Jenny Stow

When the great river goddess Yemoya sends her daughter
Aje to marry a chief in the Land of Shining Day, Aje pines
for the dark shadows of her mother's realm. So her husband sends
Crocodile and Hippopotamus down to the river to bring back a sackful of Night…
A Yoruba creation myth from West Africa that will delight young readers.

Suitable for National Curriculum English – Reading, Key Stages 1 and 2
Scottish Guidelines English Language – Reading, Levels B and C

ISBN 0-7112-1378-X £5.99

Frances Lincoln titles are available from all good bookshops.
Prices are correct at time of publication, but may be subject to change.